The PIRATE and the PIG

For Judy

PUFFIN BOOKS

Published by the Penguin Group
Penguin Books Ltd, 27 Wrights Lane, London W8 5TZ, England
Penguin Books USA Inc., 375 Hudson Street, New York, New York 10014, USA
Penguin Books Australia Ltd, Ringwood, Victoria, Australia
Penguin Books Canada Ltd, 10 Alcorn Avenue, Toronto, Ontario, Canada M4V 3B2
Penguin Books (NZ) Ltd, 182–190 Wairau Road, Auckland 10, New Zealand

Penguin Books Ltd, Registered Offices: Harmondsworth, Middlesex, England

First published by Viking 1995
Published in Puffin Books 1997
1 3 5 7 9 10 8 6 4 2

Copyright © Frank Rodgers, 1995
All rights reserved

The moral right of the author/illustrator has been asserted

Made and printed in Italy by Printers srl – Trento

FRANK RODGERS

the PIRATE and the PIG

PUFFIN BOOKS

Peg-Leg Doubloon was the captain of the pirate ship, The Jolly Rotter. His crew were the nastiest, most bad-tempered bunch on the seven seas and they made it their business to hate everybody.

But the person they hated most was Peg-Leg. They thought he wasn't nearly nasty enough to be captain.

So Peg-Leg had no friends aboard ship – except one. A pig. She had been given to him by his old mum many years before. He called the pig Matey, and he and the pig loved each other very much.

The crew hated the pig as much as they hated the captain and often called her names behind Peg-Leg's back.

"Porkchop!" they would hiss, or "Baconrind!"
or even "Sausagemeat!"

"Ship on the starboard bow!"
yelled the lookout one morning
from the crow's nest at the top of the
mast.

"Aha! More booty!" gloated the
crew.

"No lads," said Peg-Leg. "I've been
thinking about this. Why do we have
to be so nasty? We've got enough
treasure to last us for ever. There'll be
no more pirating. That's an order."

No more pirating! The nastiest crew on the seven seas couldn't believe their ears.

This was the last straw.

"If that's an order, then it's your last one!" they screamed. "We're taking over!"

The crew rushed at Peg-Leg, tied him up and locked him in his cabin.

Back on deck, they looked craftily at the other ship and licked their lips. "I'll bet it's chock-full of gold and jewels," leered Billy Blackheart, the nastiest of the bunch.

"You're dead right there, Billy," agreed Hookie, his shifty crony. "It'll be stuffed to the gunwales with treasure!"

The crew sniggered at the thought of easy spoils. "Now, lads," hissed Billy, taking command, "this is what we'll do . . . We'll put up a nice, cheery flag so they won't know we're pirates . . . we'll get as close as we can . . . then we'll pounce!"

The other ship sailed closer and closer . . .
and the pirates waited in deathly silence,
crouching over their cannons.

Matey couldn't bear the suspense any longer. She just had to go and see
if Peg-Leg was all right. With a loud "Oink!" she charged across the
deck, heading for the captain's cabin. She gave one of the crew such a
fright that he accidentally fired his cannon.

BOOM!

The other ship didn't need telling twice. "Pirates!" yelped its crew and they sailed away quicker than you can say 'slithering sea snakes!'

The crew of The Jolly Rotter were furious. "Where's that pig?" they roared. "We'll boil it alive . . . we'll slice it into a million bits . . . we'll – "

"Wait!" cried Billy Blackheart. "I've got a better idea. We could fatten up the pig and have it for Christmas dinner!"
"What a tasty idea!" cried Hookie. "And as a double treat we can make old Peg-Leg walk the plank!"

So, as the days went by, Matey was fed all the best titbits from the pirates' meals and the pirate chef cooked her extra special dinners of her own. Matey couldn't help eating everything that was put in front of her. She was a pig after all.

So Matey grew fatter and fatter and Peg-Leg grew thinner and thinner because he was just given bread and water. And all the time he worried about Matey.

atey missed the captain terribly, but didn't know what to do. All the crew were being especially nice to her, and she couldn't understand why. . .

especially on Christmas Eve, when they all came up to her with big smiles showing their rotten teeth and said things like, "My, my . . . isn't Matey looking nice? Good enough to eat!" Or, "Isn't she beautifully fat? Such a perfectly plump pig!" And they grinned in a strange way and prodded her with their dirty fingers.

Christmas Day dawned clear and bright. The ship was sailing near to the Equator so the morning was warm. The lookout scattered bits of torn paper from the crow's nest to look like snow and some of the others made a Christmas tree out of bits of old, tarry rope and seaweed.

"Now," Blackheart said, "it's time to turn that pig into our Christmas dinner." The crew cackled horribly and began to sharpen their knives. They opened the hatch that led down to the galley where Matey was having her last breakfast.

"Bring up the Christmas pig!" they yelled.

"**B**ring up the captain too!" shouted Billy Blackheart.
"That way they can say goodbye to each other before he walks the plank." He pretended to wipe away a tear. Hookie sniggered.

"What a silly old sentimental person you are," he said. "You should be called Billy Softheart!"

Matey was so fat by this time that she could hardly get through the hatch. The cook pushed from below and the crew pulled from above until suddenly Matey popped through the opening, like a cork from a bottle.

S he spotted Peg-Leg as he too was hauled on deck, and, with a squeal of delight, ran over to him. Peg-Leg looped his tied hands over her head and gave her a big hug.

"Looks like our last voyage, old girl," he said sadly.

"Stop that soppy snivelling!" yelled Billy Blackheart. "'It's time for a dip!"
The crew roared with laughter. Peg-Leg was pushed up on to the plank and
at the same time the crew closed in around Matey, knives in their
hands.

Up went the blades, all glinting in the sun.

Even the lookout was there, down from his high
perch to join in the fun. So no one noticed the
approaching danger . . . except Peg-Leg.
"Reef straight ahead!" he cried. "Abandon ship!"

Blackheart snorted. "You can't fool us with
that old trick," he laughed and moved closer
to Matey, grinning horribly.

CRASH!

The ship lurched suddenly to one side, throwing Peg-Leg off the plank.

"Don't say I didn't warn you!" he shouted as he hit the water.

"Abandon ship!" screamed the crew and rushed to the lifeboat. Matey was squealing in alarm. She had seen Peg-Leg fall overboard. Without a moment's thought she climbed up the sloping deck and dived in after him.

"Pull for your lives!"
yelled Billy Blackheart.
The pirates pulled hard on
the oars and the lifeboat
was soon far from the
sinking ship, leaving Peg-Leg
and Matey to their fate.

Peg-Leg couldn't see
Matey anywhere, and
was struggling to stay afloat.

I wish I'd learned how to swim, he thought, as he went down for the third
time. Suddenly his tied hands brushed against something that felt like a
short bit of coiled rope.

He grabbed it. It was Matey's tail!

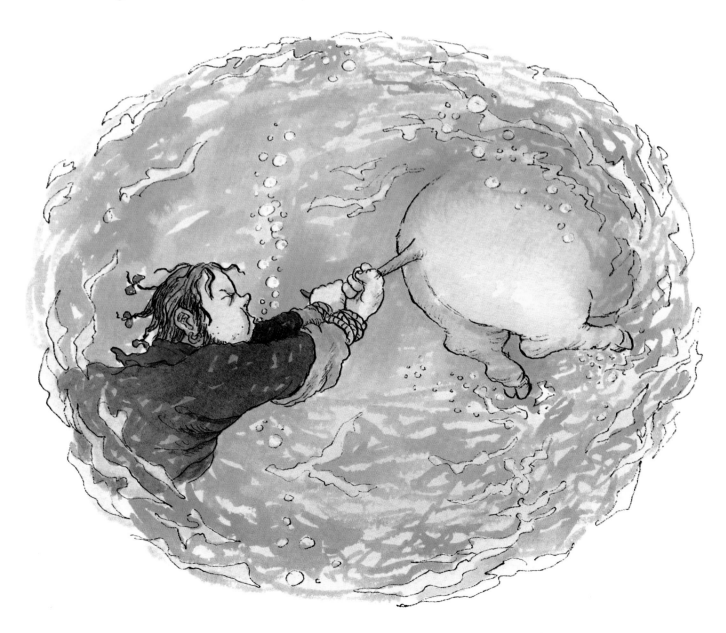

Peg-Leg was pulled to the surface and saw Matey's big fat bottom right in front of him moving steadily away from the doomed ship. He hung on tightly to Matey's tail as the big-hearted pig swam for dear life, towing her friend to safety.

Peg-Leg heard a mighty gurgle and splash behind him and knew that The Jolly Rotter had gone down.

Well, that really is the end of my pirating, he thought. And good riddance!

All that day, Matey swam and Peg-Leg hung on.
As the sun set, they reached an island and crawled thankfully up on to the beach.

The next morning, Peg-Leg and Matey were wakened by the sound of voices not far off. They crept through the palms and looked down on to the next bay.

There they saw a strange sight – the sopping wet crew of The Jolly Rotter standing in an angry crowd round Billy Blackheart!

"This is all your fault!" they shouted. "You had us rowing around in circles last night and now we're wrecked on a desert island! Marooned! I wish we had Peg-Leg back to lead us," grumbled Hookie. "He'd know what to do. You're useless!"

"Yes, utterly useless!" agreed the crew savagely. "We're going to boil your brains in a bucket of brine!"

They closed in and Billy backed off, alarmed.

It was Matey who saved Billy from a horrible fate. "Oink!" she squealed.

The crew looked up in surprise and delight.

"Matey! Captain!" they cried, and rushed to meet them.

"We'll never mutiny again, Captain," they spluttered. "Never!"

"And what's more," declared Billy Blackheart, glad that his brains were still where they should be, "I for one am going to become a vegetarian."

"And so will we!" cried the rest of the crew. "Pirates' promise!"

Peg-Leg laughed and patted Matey.

"Well, old girl . . . that's just about the nicest thing you could ever wish to hear them say, isn't it?"

Matey agreed. "Oink!" she said.